Usborne
Forgotten Fairy Tales
The
Daring Princess

Retold by Susanna Davidson
Illustrated by Alessandra Santelli

Reading consultant: Alison Kelly

About
Forgotten Fairy Tales

People have been telling each other fairy tales for thousands of years. Then, a few hundred years ago, collectors began writing the stories down. The ones that became famous were the ones that reflected the ideas of the time.

These stories had patient, polite princesses such as *Snow White* and *Sleeping Beauty*. The tales with bold girls fighting their own battles were ignored.

This series brings to life the stories of those forgotten brave and brilliant girls...

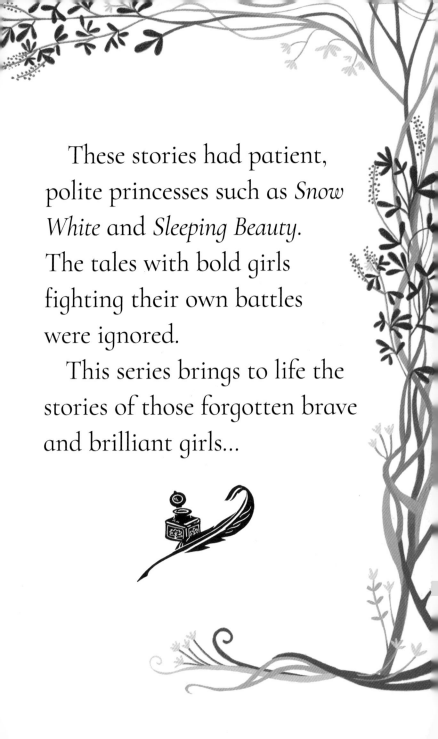

Contents

Chapter 1

Into the forest

Bessie was happiest when she was in the stables or with the blacksmith, watching him work. There was just one problem...

...Bessie was a princess, and princesses weren't *meant* to be in stables – or to spend time with blacksmiths.

"You should learn to sew," said her mother, the queen.

"And to sing," said her father, the king.

"Singing and sewing are proper princess pursuits," they chanted together.

Then her father saw the tool belt around her waist.

"From now on, there are to be no more *unprincessy* activities," snapped her mother.

"But then you're stopping me from doing everything I love," cried Bessie.

In tears, she ran out of the palace... and into the forest.

Bessie dashed down twisting paths. The sky grew darker. An owl hooted. In the distance, a wolf howled.

It wasn't long before Bessie realized she was very, very lost.

Chapter 2

The iron stove

After hours of wandering,
Bessie came to a little cottage.

It had a thatched roof
and little crooked chimneys.
Bessie knocked lightly on the
door and it swung open...

Inside, were bunches of dried
herbs. Glowing glass bottles
lined the shelves.

There was a bubbling cauldron, too, and a large iron stove.

Then Bessie heard a voice, coming from *inside* the stove.

"I'm Prince Alfred," said the voice. "Trapped here by a witch. *Please*, help me."

Bessie bent down to peer through a small crack.

Don't worry. I'll get you out!

At once, Bessie reached for her tool belt. She took out her chisel, and began to scrape away at the stove.

Finally, the hole was big enough for Prince Alfred to climb out. "Thank you," he said. "I owe you my life."

"A witch trapped me here," he explained, "until I agreed to marry her. She said only a princess could save me, but that none would dare!"

"Well I dared!" said Bessie, proudly. "You're free now."
But she spoke too soon.

"Stop!" came a loud cry.
They turned to see a witch,
with flowing red hair and a
long black cloak.

There was a rumble of thunder, and a blinding flash of light. When Bessie looked again, both the witch and the prince had vanished.

Bessie ran into the forest. "Come back!" she called. There was no answer. "I'll rescue you, Prince Alfred," she vowed.

Chapter 3

The magic chest

Bessie stumbled through the night, calling for help, until she came to a tiny house.

To her surprise, a toad answered her knock. "Come in, come in," said the toad.

The toads invited her to supper, and Bessie told them her story.

"We can help you," said the smallest toad.

He hopped over to an old chest and opened the lid, filling the room with glittering stars.

"Here are six needles, a cart wheel and three nuts," said the largest toad.

"To find the prince, you will need to cross a glass mountain, a field of swirling spikes and a great lake."

"Take these objects with you. They will help you on your journey."

"Thank you!" said Bessie.

She left at first light. Before long, she came to a towering glass mountain, sheer as ice.

"How will I ever climb it?" wondered Bessie. But then she remembered the needles.

She pierced them into
the side of the mountain,
to make steps. She did
this again and again.
Slowly, slowly,
she climbed the
mountain. It
took her all
day and into
the night.

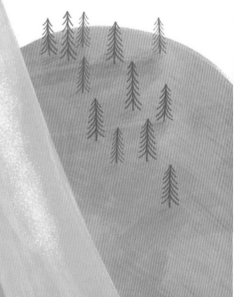

When at last she reached
the other side, Bessie fell into
a deep sleep. She woke with
the rising sun.

Bessie walked on, until she
came to the field of swirling
spikes. She untied the cart
wheel and rode it through the
spiky field.

It took her all day and into
the night. Then she curled up
beneath the stars, and slept.

On the third day, Bessie woke to the sound of lapping waves. Before her was a great lake. "What now?" she said.

Only the nuts were left. Bessie cracked one open. Inside, to her amazement, was a tiny boat, no bigger than a pea.

Bessie placed it on the water. The little boat grew and grew, until it was big enough for her to climb aboard.

Bessie sailed across the lake. Once more, it took her all day and into the night. At last, she reached a castle on the far shore.

One window was lit up
in the darkness. And there,
standing tall, with flowing
hair and a sweeping gown,
was the witch.

Chapter 4

The castle

"If the witch is here," thought Bessie, "maybe the prince is too." Bravely, she entered the castle.

She saw servants rushing along the corridors, carrying plates piled high with food.

"The witch marries the prince tonight," said a servant.

"Where can I find him?" asked Bessie.

"The door behind you leads
to a tower," said the servant.
"Keep climbing till you reach
the very top."

"Thank you," said Bessie,
and she began to climb.

At the top of the tower was a narrow room. Prince Alfred lay in bed, fast asleep. Bessie tried everything she could to wake him, but nothing worked.

Then she remembered she still had two nuts left.

Bessie cracked one open and saw a golden liquid. She let it drip onto the prince's lips.

His eyes fluttered open. "You saved me again!" he said. "Thank you! You are the most *daring* princess I've ever met."

Hand in hand, they hurried down the turret stairs and out of the castle.

There was the boat, waiting for them. They set sail across the great lake.

"Safe at last!" said Bessie.

Chapter 5

The chase

Together, Bessie and the prince crossed the field of swirling spikes and climbed the glass mountain, sheer as ice.

"My parents' castle is on the other side of this forest," said Bessie. "We're nearly home." But behind them came the witch. She had turned herself into a howling green wind.

"What do we do now?" said Prince Alfred. "We'll never outrun the witch!"

Bessie pulled the last nut from her pocket. She cracked it open. Out sprang a white stallion, pawing and snorting.

Bessie and Alfred leaped onto the stallion's back.

The witch was no match for the magical stallion. As the green wind raced after them, it grew slower and weaker.

It became a whisper, then a flutter, then a breath... Then nothing at all.

The stallion galloped all
the way to the castle. Bessie's
parents rushed out to greet
them.

When Bessie told her
parents her story, they
beamed with pride.

"And where is your home?"
the queen asked Prince Alfred.
"Beyond the glass mountain,"
the prince replied.

"After my parents died, the
witch came to our castle and
made it hers."

"She locked me in a stove
and cast a spell on my brothers
and sisters. I don't know what
happened to them."

"Well we've defeated the witch," said Bessie. "And together, we can search for your brothers and sisters."

The next day, the king and queen threw a party to celebrate.

Everyone in the kingdom was invited. One family looked strangely familiar.

They all smiled at Bessie and shook her hand. But when they saw the prince, they rushed into his arms.

"My brothers and sisters!" cried Prince Alfred. "Where have you been?"

"The witch turned us all into toads," said the eldest sister. She looked at Bessie. "When you freed our brother, you broke her spell."

"Three cheers for the daring princess!" cried Prince Alfred.

Everyone raised their glasses and cheered, "To the daring princess. Hip hip hooray!"

About the story

The Daring Princess is based on a fairy tale called *The Iron Stove*, which was first published by the Brothers Grimm, Jacob and Wilhelm, over two hundred years ago.

Andrew and Nora Lang also included the story

in *The Yellow Fairy Book*, which was first published in 1894.

This story is different from many popular fairy tales, as it has a princess who rescues a prince.

Designed by Laura Bridges
Series designer: Russell Punter
Series editor: Lesley Sims

First published in 2021 by Usborne Publishing Ltd.,
Usborne House, 83-85 Saffron Hill, London EC1N 8RT, England.
usborne.com Copyright © 2021, 2019 Usborne Publishing Ltd.